D1341775

Race Ahead with Reading

The Big Bad Wolf and the Robot Pig

By Laura North

Illustrated by Kevin Cross

W
FRANKLIN WATTS
LONDON•SYDNEY

Chapter 1

"I'll huff and I'll puff and I'll blow

your house down!" cried the Wolf.

"Huff!

Puff!

Huff! Puff! Huff..."

"You can't get us Mr Wolf!"
squealed the Three Little Pigs.
"You're hairy and scary.
But we're too clever for you!"

In fact, only one of
the pigs was clever.

One pig was very lazy.

The third was very greedy.

Clever Pig had knocked down
the straw and wood houses. He built
their new houses from strong steel,
with hi-tech security systems.

"Huff!

Puff!

Wheeze!"

The Wolf huffed and puffed

until he was panting.

"I give up," he said.

He walked away with his tail

between his legs.

That evening, he sat at his

dinner table with nothing to eat.

"I can't scare the pigs any more.

That means no more bacon,

sausages or ham."

Just the thought of it made the

Wolf hungry. He licked his lips.

"I have to get those pigs!"

Suddenly, the Wolf had an idea.

Chapter 2

"If I can't get into the pigs' houses,"
said the Wolf, "I will make
them come to me!"

The Wolf got to work at once. He hammered
and banged, and sparks flew everywhere!
He used tin cans and an egg carton.

He worked all night until, finally,

his creation was ready.

"I will call him Robot Pig,"

said the Wolf.

"Robot Pig will knock on the Three Little Pigs' doors and invite them to a tea party at my house. He will be the perfect trap." laughed the Wolf.

"Hmm... he doesn't look much like a pig," the Wolf worried.

"I know!" he cried. He went to the cupboard

and got out a big tin of pink paint.

"This will do the trick," he said, pouring

paint all over the metal creature.

Then the Wolf got out a remote control
and pressed a big red button.

"Oink!" said the Pig.
"Hello Master!"

"Eureka!" shouted the Wolf.
"It works!"

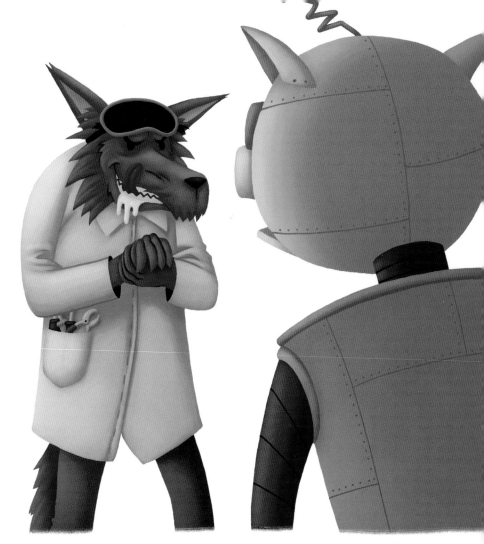

The Wolf looked at the Robot Pig, hungrily.

"If you weren't made out of tin cans,

I would eat you all up."

He smiled, licking his lips.

Chapter 3

Zzzzz. Lazy Pig was having a sleep
when there was a knock at his door.

"Who is it?" asked Lazy Pig, frightened.

"I am your new neighbour,"

said the Robot Pig.

"Phew, it's just a big pig!

I thought it might be the Wolf

trying to eat me." sighed Lazy Pig.

He took the chains off the door and

opened the bolts. The door swung open.

"Hello," said the Robot Pig.

"I would like to invite you

to a tea party this afternoon."

"Oh," yawned Lazy Pig,

"I really do have a lot of sleeping to do."

"There will be a big bed full of

soft straw and fluffy pillows."

added Robot Pig.

"In that case, count me in!"

said Lazy Pig.

17

Next Robot Pig knocked at the door
of Greedy Pig.

"Hello. Please come to my party.
There will be huge plates of cakes, jelly
and ice-cream, and jugs of cream."

"Yes, yes, yes!"

said Greedy Pig, drooling.

"I'll be there!"

"My plan is working perfectly!" whispered

the Wolf, peering out from behind a bush.

Finally, Robot Pig knocked on
the door of Clever Pig's house.
"We are holding a tea party for all
the cleverest pigs in the country.
Will you be our guest of honour?"

Clever Pig was easily flattered.
"Of course!" he said, proudly.

The Wolf smiled, flashing two rows

of pointy yellow teeth.

"What a feast I will have, tasty pigs

for starter, main course and dessert!"

Chapter 4

"Knock! Knock! Knock!" The Wolf heard

the sound of trotters tapping on his door.

Three juicy little pigs were outside.

"I don't need to go out for dinner,"

said the Wolf, "I've got room service."

The Wolf picked up the remote control.

Robot Pig rolled to the front door as

Wolf hid behind the cupboard.

"Welcome to my tea party," said Robot Pig.

"Do come in."

There was one big, empty plate

in the middle of the table.

"Where's the bed?" asked Lazy Pig.

"Where's the food?" asked Greedy Pig.

"Where are all the clever pigs?"

asked Clever Pig.

"Have something to eat," said Robot Pig.

The Clever Pig looked more closely
at Robot Pig.

"You're painted pink!" he said.
"We've been tricked!"

"Yes," said the Wolf as he jumped out

from behind the cupboard.

"It's time for my tea!"

He chased them round the table.

"Squeal!" cried the pigs.

Chapter Five

The Wolf was just about take a big bite

out of Greedy Pig when Clever Pig

noticed something.

"The Wolf has left the remote control

by the front door," he thought.

He picked it up in his trotters and

pressed the big red button in the middle.

"OINK! OINK! OINK!" said Robot Pig.

Clever Pig pushed the lever forward.

Robot Pig rolled towards the Wolf.

"What's happening?" the Wolf cried.

"OINK! OINK! OINK!"

roared Robot Pig.

The Wolf looked up in terror.

"Stop!" he cried.

"I'm your master, remember?"

"You're hairy and scary,"

said Robot Pig.

"Argggh!" screamed the Wolf

and he ran out of the house.

Robot Pig whizzed after him

on his super fast robo wheels.

"That Robot Pig saved our bacon,"

said Greedy Pig.

"This is a nice house, isn't it?"

said Clever Pig.

"Yes," said Lazy Pig.

"We could be very comfortable here."

Outside, Robot Pig chased the Wolf

over the hills and out of the village,

never to return.

First published in 2012 by
Franklin Watts
338 Euston Road
London
NW1 3BH

Franklin Watts Australia
Level 17/207 Kent Street
Sydney
NSW 2000

Text © Laura North 2012
Illustration © Kevin Cross 2012

The rights of Laura North to be
identified as the author and Kevin Cross
as the illustrator of this Work have been
asserted in accordance with the Copyright,
Designs and Patents Act, 1988.

Series Editor: Melanie Palmer
Series Advisor: Catherine Glavina
Series Designer: Peter Scoulding

A CIP catalogue record for this book is
available from the British Library.

ISBN 978 1 4451 0777 6 (hbk)
ISBN 978 1 4451 0783 7 (pbk)

Printed in China

Franklin Watts is a division of Hachette
Children's Books, an Hachette UK company.
www.hachette.co.uk